BRAND SPANKING NEW!

DOUG'S™
Hoop
Nightmare

Created by Jim Jinkins

Adapted by
Sue Kassirer

Illustrated by
Pete List and Cheng-li Chan, Tony
Curanaj, Chris Dechert, Brian Donnelly,
Ray Feldman, Chris Palesty, Matt
Peters, and Jonathan Royce

Disney
PRESS

New York

Original Script by Scott Fellows

Original Characters for "The Funnies"
Developed by Jim Jinkins and Joe Aaron

Library of Congress Catalog Card Number: 96-71634

ISBN:0-7868-4188-5

Chapter 1

Dear Journal, It's me, Doug. Well, it finally happened. School is finally out! I decided the best way to have a great summer was to get super-organized. So I set up this schedule:

10:00 A.M.: Wake up.
10:15: Feed Porkchop. (That's my dog.)

10:30: Feed myself.

10:35: Burp.

10:50: Watch TV.

11:30: Feed self some more. Something good this time, like banana pudding or pizza.

11:35: Burp.

12:00 noon: Goof off at Skeeter's. (He's my best friend.)

Woops! I looked at my watch and saw that it was already 12:05 and I was still swallowing my pizza. Hadn't even burped yet. Somehow I'd gotten behind schedule. Must have been the cool show I was watching on TV.

So I beelined it over to Skeet's house and rang the bell. And that's when my super-organized summer hit snag number one.

"Sorry, Doug," said Mrs. Valentine. "Skeeter had to rush off this morning. He was accepted last night to Camp Einstein. He said he'd see you in two weeks."

"Camp Einstein?" I said with my mouth hanging open.

How could my best friend do this to me? Sure, he was smart and everything. But what a bum thing to do! Leave for some genius camp without saying good-bye to his best friend!

I kind of slumped away and headed for my two o'clock: visit the Sleech twins and check out their new computer advances.

When I knocked on their door their dad answered.

"They just left for Virtual Camp," he said.

Virtual Camp? Man, what was the world coming to? Camp Einstein, Virtual Camp. Don't kids ever stay home and just goof off in the summer?

I decided to go to Swirly's and hang out for a while. I ordered a shake and french fries and pulled out my schedule. The only other thing I'd written down was:

4:00: Avoid Roger.

3

So of course he showed up—and started sticking his nose into my business.

"What're you doin' here, Funnie?" he said, and scowled. "Did ya miss the bus to Camp Wetabed, or what? You gonna finish those?" He grabbed a fistful of french fries.

"Help yourself, Roger," I said as he stuffed his face.

It seemed like Roger Klotz was the only kid left in town. And believe me, he's the one kid you don't want to mess with. If there were a Camp Bully, he would have left town, too, I'm sure.

With everyone but Roger away, what was I supposed to do all summer?

Chapter 2

As it turned out, Mom had some ideas.

"Doug," she said at dinner, "since all your friends are off to camp, maybe you'd like to go, too." *Plunk!* She dumped all these camp brochures next to my plate.

"They're fun and educational," added Dad.

Oh no, I thought. The fun part sounded okay. But educational?

"What do you say, son?" asked Dad with an earnest look on his face.

"Thanks, Mom and Dad, but I just don't think I'm the summer camp kinda guy," I said.

At least, that's what I thought—until the doorbell rang, and in jogged Patti Mayonnaise.

So, Journal, I guess I haven't told anybody but you about Patti yet. Well, let me put it simply. Just thinking about her makes my breath get short and my heart thump real hard. You know. Like in the comic books. Little hearts around my head and everything. But this is for real.

"Hi, Patti!" I said in a real breathless

voice. "Want to have some dinner?"

"Can't, Doug. I'm in training," she said. She was breathless, too, but that's because she was still jogging, even while we spoke. "I'm going to sports camp tomorrow."

I couldn't believe it. Even Patti was going to camp? My heart slowed down real quick and all the little hearts around my head sorta melted.

"I just wanted to return your Smash

Adams videotape. Too bad you're not goin'.
We'd have a lot of fun. Well, see you in two
weeks."

With that, Patti jogged off.

I could deal with Skeeter and the Sleech
twins being away for the next two weeks. But
Patti Mayonnaise? This was more than I
could take.

I knew I had to act—and fast. So what if

I wasn't exactly Mr. Jock. So what if the word "gym" made me get weak in the knees. The truth was, I would do anything to spend two weeks with Patti Mayonnaise. Absolutely anything.

Suddenly, Camp Grinning Bear seemed like a great way to spend the next two weeks.

So that's just what I decided to do. And that's when the trouble began. . . .

Chapter 3

Mom and Dad were pleased as punch. Sure, they were a little shocked that I'd changed my mind so quickly. But they got over that real fast. After all, camp had been their idea in the first place. So I just let them think they had talked me into it.

The next day tons of school buses were lined up, ready to take all of us kids away.

"Now, don't forget to write, use sunblock, and wear eye protection," said Mom as she placed these cool mirrored sports glasses on my nose.

"And don't forget," added Dad, "to have a good time. Go get 'em, Air Funnie!" he said with a sporty punch on my arm.

I climbed onto the bus, looked around, and stopped short. This must be a bus for older kids, I thought. They all looked like giants! They all looked so serious. And what was worse, everyone was staring at me.

I started backing off. "Ah, I think I got on the wrong bus," I muttered.

That's when I heard Patti calling my name.

"Yoo hoo, Doug, over here!" she called out from the back of the bus.

So I had been wrong. It was the right bus. The bus with the giants on it. The bus to Camp Grinning Bear. The bus with Patti Mayonnaise on it. The bus I had to get on.

And that's what I did. I made my way to the back, past the giants and the stares. And I breathed a sigh of relief when I finally reached Patti and settled into the seat next to her.

Then we were off.

As we drove along into the countryside, I began to relax. Just think, I told myself. Two whole weeks with Patti Mayonnaise. What

13

could be better? So what if I couldn't throw a ball super-hard or run bases really fast? I was sure there'd be stuff to do there, like canoeing with Patti, or even hiking with Patti!

The bus screeched to a sudden halt, and I was startled by a loud voice coming over a bullhorn.

"Wake up, people! C'mon. Move it, move it, move it!"

It was a voice I would hear many times over the next two weeks. A voice I thought I had left behind. The voice of Coach Spitz, the meanest coach in the world!

Oh man, I thought. Not Spitz! Not during summer vacation!

"Doug, get your stuff!" yelled Patti. "Hurry!"

I had to run to keep up with her as she raced over to this long lineup of kids. We all stood there facing Spitz, who was barking at us like a drill sergeant.

14

"The name is Spitz, Coach Spitz," he yelled, just in case someone didn't know. "If you want to play at Camp Grinning Bear, you will play by the rules. If you don't, well, I will consider you, er . . . a non-rule-playing-type-person."

Then he walked down the line of kids and stopped right in front of me.

"What are these, Funnie?" he yelled as he

pointed a beefy finger at my sunglasses. "You think you're a movie star? Is that what you think?"

"Uh, no . . . ?" I mumbled as Spitz grabbed the glasses off my face and plunked them onto his bulbous nose.

"Let me make one thing clear, Funnie," he said as he peered at me through my shades. "The only stars in this camp will be me and my assistant coaches, Patti . . . er Mayonnaise and er . . . Chalky Studebaker."

Oh no, I thought. He's even worse at camp than he is at school. What did I get myself into here? All because of Patti Mayonnaise.

"Now, campers," Spitz continued, "you have fifteen minutes to stow your gear and regroup on the obstacle course. Move it!"

I couldn't grab my gear fast enough. Two weeks with this guy? I didn't know if I could stand it. The only thing that made the thought bearable was that I'd see Patti every day. Each and every day. I just kept telling myself that.

Especially when Spitz stopped me and yelled, "Hold it, movie star. I want you to hit the pool and give me twenty laps. Now!"

So that's what I did. I dropped my gear and headed to the pool. By myself. Without Patti Mayonnaise. And as I swam I just kept asking myself, What am I doing here? And why am I swimming with all my clothes on?

Chapter 4

The rest of that first day wasn't much better. I even thought of calling my parents to come and rescue me. But the more I thought about it the more I didn't want to get them worried. You know how parents can be. So I wrote a letter I was sure they would be happy to get.

Dear Mom and Dad,
Camp is great. The first day
we went rowing, swimming, rock
climbing, and lifesaving. Then
after lunch we trained for the

big basketball game against the
camp across the lake. I keep
seein' a lot of Patti, but I
haven't had a chance to talk
to her.

Sincerely,
Doug (your son)

We really did go swimming. We had to after
the boat capsized. And we did do some rock
climbing. We had to after we washed up on
the shores of Pointy Rock Island. I got a ton
of lifesaving tips from the paramedics. That
rescue ambula-copter was cool!

After lunch, I went back to my cabin to
rest my weary bones. It sure felt great to lie
down on my bunk—even if it did sag in the
middle. That's when I met Leonard, my bunkmate. Just as I was about to close my eyes, a
head poked down from the bunk above. Next
thing I knew, this guy leaps down, rolls up a
sleeve and tries to flex his biceps.

19

"What a workout, huh?" he says in a very husky voice. "I can feel the burn. Name's Leonard. Whaddya say?"

"I wanna go home," I mumbled.

"What was that? *Shhh . . . ,*" said Leonard.

Then he took out an asthma inhaler, put it in his mouth, and squirted.

He said, "This is my fourth sports camp this summer, ya know. I've broken out of all of 'em, and I'm bustin' outta this one, too, . . . tonight!"

Was this guy for real?

Then he got out this map he'd drawn. It said OPERATION MOO MOO on it in big letters.

Man, I thought. This is bad. Camp Grinning Bear was a lot tougher than I thought.

"Spitz may be the toughest coach around," Leonard continued as he ducked into a locker, "but he's never had to take on Leonard Fitzhugh Persimmons. Take a look at this!"

I turned my head and gaped. There was Leonard in a cow costume. Yes, a cow costume.

"Made it out of old baseball mitts," he

said, like it was the most normal thing in the world to do. "I got room in the rear, if you're interested in escaping, too."

"Ummm . . ." was all I could manage to get out.

"Suit yourself, sport boy," he said as he smacked me on the back and made his way out of the cabin.

All I could think was, Twenty laps, capsized boat, climbing rocks, helicopter rescue, and now a bunkmate who's dressed like a cow!

Chapter 5

The next day we started on real heavy-duty training. Turned out our big rival was Camp All-Star. And they didn't have that name for nothing.

Not only had they won the Inter-camp Basketball Shoot-out every year since 1902, but each camper got his own personal trainer, a high-tech workout room, and free sessions with sports psychologists. I'm not kidding.

On top of that, their coach was the one and only, legendary Coach Piney Ziggler. I heard that this guy would sell his own

grandmother to beat our team.

As for us, we had Spitz. No personal trainer. No workout room. No sports psychologists. Just fruit. Dead, ripe fruit. You heard me right.

Spitz's big method of training was to have us squeeze fruit. For some reason that was Coach Spitz's idea on how to motivate us. He figured that if we could squeeze the fruit real hard and make it splatter all over the place, we could do the same thing to the All-Stars. Or something like that.

At least we thought that was what the fruit squeezing was all about. As it turned out there was something else. Only Spitz wouldn't tell us what it was. All he would whisper was, "I got a super secret weapon that will finally bring us victory over Piney Ziggler and Camp All-Star!"

Chapter 6

"A secret weapon?" said Chalky.

"*Shhh,*" said Spitz. Then he stuck his head out the cabin door and looked around suspiciously.

"I'm not going to reveal that 'til the night of the big game!" he whispered in case someone might be listening. "Y'know, spies."

Man, I thought. This place is unbelievable. I thought I was just going to sports camp. Then it turns out my bunkmate is trying to escape like he's in jail or something. And now it turns out the coach has a secret weapon. And he's sure there are spies all over the place. This camp was getting crazier by the minute.

Even I started getting paranoid. Maybe there are spies, I thought. Take Leonard. Maybe he wasn't really trying to escape. Maybe it was all a cover. Maybe he was sneaking over to the other camp in a cow disguise and feeding them information about the secret weapon, whatever it was!

I decided to keep a real close eye on him from then on. Maybe I wasn't any good at sports. But if I could turn in a spy, at least I could show Patti I was good at something.

That night at the camp mess hall I finally got a chance to sit by Patti.

"You showed a lot of heart today in prac-

tice, Doug," she said as we sat down to eat.
"I bet the coach uses you in the big game."

"Yeah, Funnie," said Percy Femur, this
gargantuan tough guy who makes Roger
Klotz look like a wimp. "You can keep the
bench warm. Heh, heh, heh . . ."

Percy was so funny I forgot to laugh.

"That's not fair, Percy," said Patti. "Doug
might not be tallest or strongest . . . or most
coordinated, or naturally gifted—"

"All right, all right," I said. "He gets the point."

"But with practice and teamwork he knows he can do anything," finished Patti.

"It's gonna take more than that to beat Camp All-Star," said Percy as he stuffed a whole chicken in his mouth. "They have the 'killer instinct,' and they never let any puny people in."

29

"Hey, how do you know so much about Camp All-Star?" asked Chalky.

"One word," answered Percy. "Shut up."

Patti and I shot each other a glance. We knew Percy pretty well. But there was something different about him. We just weren't sure what.

Chapter 7

I was convinced things couldn't get any worse. But as I was putting my dinner mess hall tray away I heard a voice calling me.

"Doug . . . Doug . . ."

I turned around quickly. Leonard's head was sticking out of a trash can.

"Leonard?" I said.

"Just wanted to say good-bye before I put Operation Trash Dash into action," he said.

"What happened to Operation Moo Moo?" I asked.

"Ever been milked?" said Leonard with a shrug. "It ain't pretty. But now, I'm talking trash!"

Oh man, I thought. Now he's trying to escape with the trash. Unless . . . Could it be true? Could he really be a spy? My bunkmate? It really gave me the creeps just thinking about it.

I finally decided to quit worrying about Leonard and come up with my own secret plan: Operation Impress Patti. I was determined to prove to her that I was more than some loser benchwarmer.

I imagined myself driving to the basket,

hitting layups, spinning, sliding, slamming, and hitting a hook shot. And all the time Patti's looking on admiring me.

So at practice the next day I took that hook shot. And it landed in the basket. The trash basket next to the court.

I tried a spin move and release. And shattered the equipment shed window.

I heaved one over my head. And knocked a fancy hat off an old lady. Who turned out to be Leonard in another disguise.

Worst of all, you can bet who saw all this. Patti. Coach Patti. Patti Mayonnaise.

"Gee, Doug, I think we need to work on your accuracy a bit," she said.

"Really?" I said. "In what way?"

"Well," she said, "one of the most accurate ways to shoot is underhanded."

Then she took the ball in both hands, bent down low with her hands hanging to her knees, and shot the ball right into the basket.

"Try it, Doug," she said.

So I tried it. And sure enough, the ball landed in the basket.

"All right! See, Doug, you make it look easy," Patti said.

"Yeah, but it doesn't look cool," I said. "I look like a doof!" I didn't know which was worse. Looking like a loser or trying to look good and missing all the time.

34

"It went in the basket, Doug," said Patti. "What's cooler than that?"

Just at that moment Chalky showed up, grabbed the ball and shouted, "Hey, Patti! Check this out!" and he slam-dunked the ball like an all-pro.

"That was slammin', Chalky," yelled Patti as she dribbled the ball back to me.

"Here, Doug," she said. "Keep practicing. Before y'know it, you'll be sinking 'em left and right."

So I kept practicing . . . and practicing . . . and practicing. Not underhanded, of course. I was going for cool.

"Doug, that's the eighth time you missed that shot," said Patti. "Why won't you shoot the ball like we practiced?"

"'Cause I look like a doof that way," I said.

Then Mr. Know-it-All Studebaker had to put in his two bits. "Doug," he said as he spun the ball on his finger, "you can't expect

to hit baskets without practice. You've got to work at it."

"That's easy for you to say, Mr. I'm-such-a-natural-superstar-so-I-hog-the-ball-all-the-time," I shouted at him.

"What's he talking about?" said Chalky. "I don't hog the ball."

"Well," said Patti, "you do take a lot of shots."

"I do?" said Chalky. He really sounded shocked, like his feelings were hurt.

But I was so ticked off, I wasn't gonna worry about him. "Doug," said Patti, "the point is—"

I snapped at Patti, "The point is, you know I'm not going to get to play in the big game anyway. So you can just stop babying me. See ya tomorrow . . . coach."

Then I really can't believe what I did next. I turned my back on Patti and stormed off.

Chapter 8

The next day was the big game. But when I woke up I was more worried about what I'd said to Patti than about whether or not I'd

play. Or whether or not I'd make a fool of myself.

On top of everything else, that was the day that Leonard really went off the deep end. He dressed up as a plumber and said he was going to escape through the sewer lines. "It's Operation Royal Flush," he said, holding up a toilet plunger. "Wanna come?"

I have to admit, I was tempted. Even if he really was a spy. But duty called. "Thanks for the offer, Leonard. But I think I'll stick around," I said. "I did something kinda dumb yesterday, and I think I'll try and patch things up."

"Well, your loss," said Leonard with a shrug. "If you see Spitz, tell him I'm real sorry I missed the big game," he added with a big wheezy laugh as he took off on his bike.

I took off, too, for the big game. For better or for worse.

Man, the bleachers were packed. I think everyone from the tri-county area came to

39

watch us play that day.

And no one looked better than the Camp All-Star team. They had the look of victory. And our team looked like . . . well . . . not so good. Everybody looked a little green around the gills, like they were going to lose it any minute.

Of course Mr. Compassionate, Coach Spitz, couldn't believe what was happening to his team. "You guys can't be sick," he said.

He pulled out some bottles of juice from his satchel. They were filled with his homemade Liquid Spitz.

"Here, you need to drink more Liquid Spitz!" he said, and handed the bottles around. But at that, everyone ran off holding their mouths. And in a few seconds I heard the sound of all the toilets flushing at once.

"Man, what's going on?" I said.

"Femur," yelled Spitz. "How come you're not in the john?"

"Because I didn't drink that crud," said Percy.

"Me neither," I added.

"Not me," said Patti. "You musta given it out while we were practicing. What is it, anyhow?"

"What is it?" said Spitz. "It's my secret weapon!"

Chapter 9

It turned out that Spitz had revealed his secret weapon the day before while Patti, Chalky, and I were busy practicing.

During the morning fruit-squeezing session Spitz had opened a big crate that said SECRET WEAPON on it. It held hundreds of bottles of this gross drink called Liquid Spitz. And it turned out that this stuff was made of the juice of all the fruit we'd been squeezing since we'd arrived.

"It was supposed to make us win," grumbled Spitz. "But . . . er . . . ." He scratched his head.

"Something musta gone wrong with the formula."

"Who else didn't drink the 'liquid crud'?" he barked.

"Me," said Chalky.

"Great!" yelled Spitz. "That gives us one, two, three, four. . . ." He counted as he pointed to Patti, Percy, Chalky, and me.

"Looks like we're gonna have to forfeit, coach," said Percy. He didn't sound too upset, either. It was like the guy didn't care if we lost or won. "Too bad you don't have one more player."

That's when we heard a shriek.

"Ahhhhhhhhhhhhhhhhh!"

Someone came bursting out of a sewer manhole in an overflowing tide of green liquid. It was Leonard. Who else? He had been trying to escape.

"Hellooooo!" shrieked Spitz. "Point guard!"

Chapter 10

So, Journal, I couldn't believe it. There I was, starting in the big game. That meant that I had one last chance to prove to Patti I could shoot!

But the first half didn't go so well. Leonard just froze in the middle of the court. And instead of shooting the ball, Chalky kept passing it.

Uh-oh, I thought. That must be because I called him a ball hog. But if Chalky doesn't start shooting, we don't stand a chance.

Then there was Percy. He was playing

even worse than me. I mean, he kept passing the ball to All-Star players.

Suddenly it clicked. Percy was the spy—of course! Percy didn't drink the Liquid Spitz. He knew more about the other team than anyone. And now he was trying to help them win. It all made sense. And now that I thought about it, he sure fit the part.

And Leonard was innocent! Leonard

really and truly just wanted to escape from camp.

I was proud of myself for figuring out about Percy. Gotta tell Coach later, I thought. But in the meantime, all I wanted to do was hit a basket without looking stupid.

So I tried a hook shot. But it went flying into the bleachers!

At halftime the score was thirty-four to twelve. And you can guess who was winning. Something had to be done. But what?

Coach Spitz sure didn't have a clue. And

he sure didn't look happy about it. Neither did we. The only one who looked happy was Percy. He kept on smiling like it was all some big joke or something.

"Studebaker," Spitz said. "Try shooting the ball. And Percy, why don't you try a little harder to give the game away."

"Doin' my best, Coach," Percy answered.

No joke, I thought.

"And Mayonnaise," Spitz added, "some assistant coach you turned out to be!"

That was more than I could take. I couldn't stand to hear him talk that way to Patti. I knew what I had to do.

"Wait!" I said. "Don't blame Patti, Coach. It's . . . it's really all my fault."

"I know, Funnie, but wait your turn," said Spitz.

"No, I mean, this is all my fault. I called Chalky a ball hog. And he's not. He's the best player I've ever seen. And I guess I was just jealous. . . ."

Chalky raised his head for the first time that day.

"And Patti . . . Patti is the best assistant coach a guy could have. She taught me that it takes a lot of practice to be good at something, and twice as much if you're not."

I paused, and Patti gave me a smile that made the last two weeks worth everything that had gone wrong.

"And we've practiced twice as hard as Camp All-Star. That's why we can still go out there and beat 'em! Now who's with me?"

My answer was silence—except for another round of toilet flushing.

"Yeah, okay," said Spitz as he wandered off toward the bathroom. "There's nothin' else better to do."

"I thought it was a nice speech, Doug," said Patti.

"It was beautiful, man," said Percy. He was all misty-eyed. What a shock!

"Let's play some ball!" I shouted.

"Let's go!" yelled Chalky.

So what do you know? My speech really worked.

Chapter 11

In the second half, Chalky was his old self again. He was scoring points left and right. Patti even got Leonard in the game with her no-look pass. He had no choice. The ball bounced off his head and into the basket!

No one could believe Percy's new winning attitude. I guess he decided it was more fun to win for his team than to be a spy after all.

Even I tried another shot. And missed. Which made me decide to pass the ball for the rest of the game. At least that was safe.

Or I thought it was. Until one of the All-Star players fouled me. Now I had to shoot the ball whether I wanted to or not.

I walked to the foul line and the ref handed me the ball.

"You have two shots, son," he said.

I looked up at the scoreboard. It said, 00:02 LEFT, ALL-STARS: 51, THE BEARS: 50.

I stood there frozen. I closed my eyes. I could see it. A big fancy digital scoreboard, like the ones in the big games. The commentator says, "Funnie at the line. The Bears trail by one. Oh no, he's going to shoot the ball underhanded. He looks soooo stupid." All these giant pro-basketball players were laughing and pointing their fingers at me.

But I quickly snapped back to reality. 'Cause I knew something had to be done.

It's just a game, I told myself. And win or lose, I want to go out with style, right?

So I shot the ball overhand. The ball hit the rim, but missed. "Yeah!" screamed the All-Stars. My team was silent.

That's when the truth hit me. I was trying so hard not to look stupid that I was letting my team down.

I looked over and spotted Patti. Boy, did she look defeated. And all I ever wanted to do was impress her, right? Maybe if I had just listened to her I would have been better off.

I made up my mind. Here goes nothin', I told myself. I took a deep breath. And I bent down and set the ball between my legs.

I thought I heard some of the All-Stars laugh. I'm really not sure. All I had on my

mind at that moment was getting that ball through the hoop and scoring the point that would tie the game.

And that's exactly what I did.

"IT'S GOOD!" yelled Spitz. The scoreboard read 00:00, ALL STARS: 51, THE BEARS: 51.

"Overtime!" screamed the referee.

In overtime, the whole team pulled together and played hard. The final score was All-Stars: 56, The Bears: 62.

Ol' Grinning Bear really showed Camp All-Star that with practice and teamwork, you can do anything!

The crowd cheered like crazy. And Patti, Chalky, and I got a free ride—on Percy's shoulders.

So Percy turned out to be a pretty lousy spy for the other team but a great player on our team. And I'd been wrong to suspect poor Leonard.

Just as I was thinking about him, Patti

yelled out, "Hey, look over there!"

"So he finally did it!" I shouted as I turned and saw my bunkmate, dressed like a Swirly's ice cream guy, riding his bike right through the crowd and out the main gate.

At least I thought it was my bunkmate, until Leonard came slumping toward us with his fists pounding the air.

"Hey, that guy just stole my bike!" he screamed over and over.

"Come on up here, Len," I finally said. "After all, without you we never would have qualified to play today!" With that, Percy hoisted him up with the rest of us. And for the first time in two weeks, Leonard smiled.

"And without you, Doug, we never would have won!" said Patti.

Well, Journal, I guess I don't need to tell

you how great that made me feel. Let's just say that all those little hearts around my head that had been melting came back bigger and brighter than ever before.

GET A **FREE** ISSUE OF

The fun-filled magazine that kids enjoy and parents applaud.

A whopping one million kids ages 7 to 14 are dedicated to reading Disney Adventures—you will be, too!

Each month DA plugs kids into super-charged fun...

- The inside scoop on movie stars and athletes
- Hot, new video games and how to beat 'em
- The characters they love
- Stories about everyday kids
- *PLUS:* puzzles, contests, trivia, comics, and much, much more!

- -

☐ **YES!** Send me a FREE issue of **DISNEY ADVENTURES MAGAZINE.**
(If my child loves it) I pay only $14.95 for the next 11 issues (12 in all). I save over $20 off the cover price. If we decide not to subscribe, I'll return the bill marked "cancel" and owe nothing. The FREE issue is ours to keep.

Mail your order to: DISNEY ADVENTURES
PO BOX 37284
Boone, IA 50037-0284

Child's Name _____ Birthday (optional):_____

Address _____

City _____ State _____ Zip _____

Parent's Signature _____

Payment enclosed _____ Bill me _____

Canadian and Foreign orders, please add $10 for postage and GST.
First issue will arrive within 4-8 weeks. Regular cover price is $2.99 per issue.

@ Disney   L1H1

Notes:

My Doodle Page: